For Greg Pizzoli
M B

For Mila Jane and Mason
S H

First published 2020 by Walker Books Ltd
87 Vauxhall Walk, London SE11 5HJ

2 4 6 8 10 9 7 5 3 1

Text © 2020 Mac Barnett
Illustrations © 2020 Shawn Harris

The right of Mac Barnett and Shawn Harris to be identified as author and illustrator respectively
of this work has been asserted by them in accordance with the Copyright,
Designs and Patents Act 1988

This book has been typeset in Rockwell

Printed in China

British Library Cataloguing in Publication Data:
a catalogue record for this book is available from the British Library

ISBN 978-1-4063-9507-5

www.walker.co.uk

WALKER BOOKS
AND SUBSIDIARIES
LONDON • BOSTON • SYDNEY • AUCKLAND

A Polar Bear in the Snow

MAC BARNETT

ART BY **SHAWN HARRIS**

There is a polar bear in the snow.

Still asleep,
he lifts his nose
to sniff the air –

and he awakens.

There is a polar bear in the snow.

Where is he going?

Is he going to visit the seals?

No. He is not hungry.

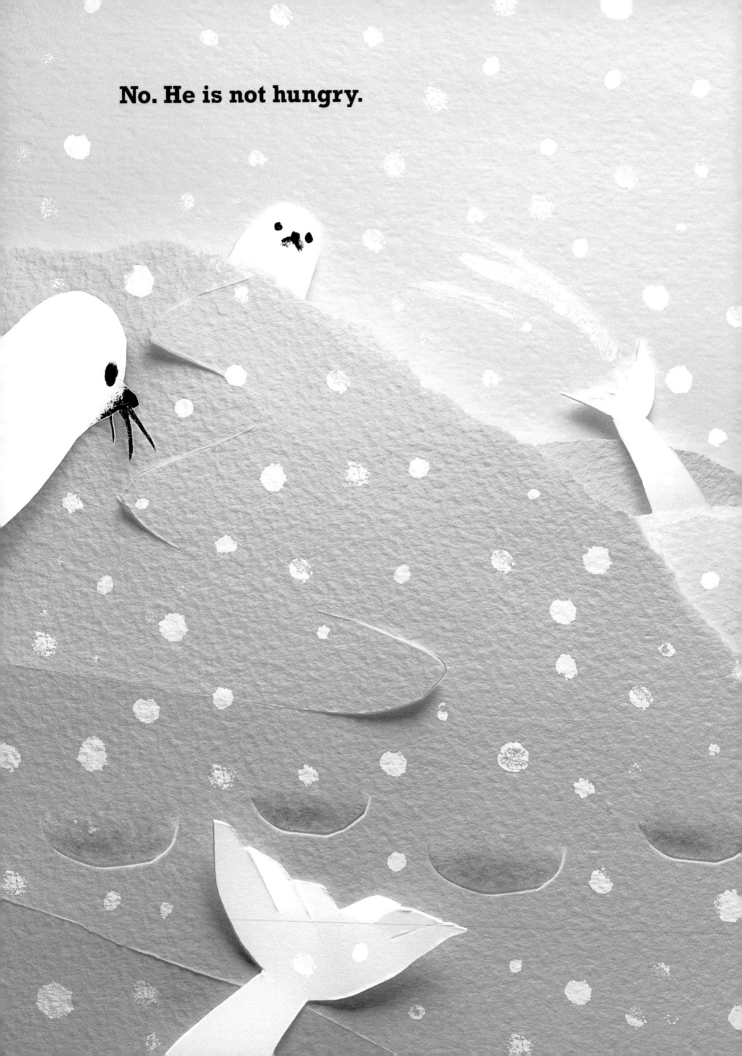

Is he going to hunker in a cave?

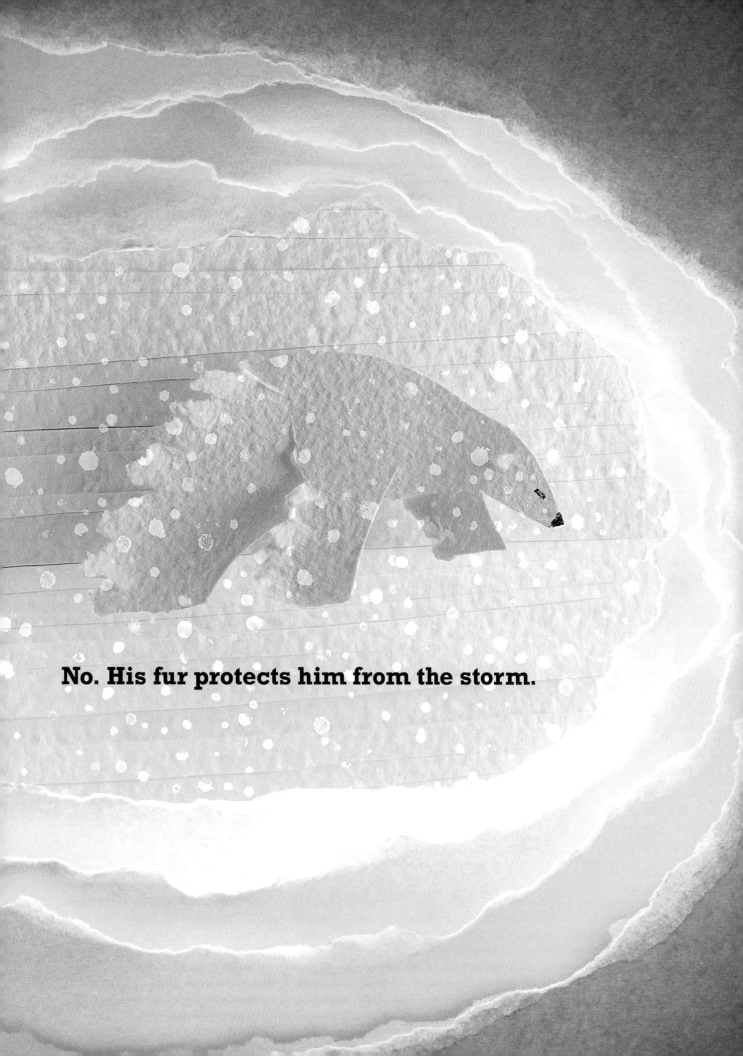

No. His fur protects him from the storm.

Is he going to meet a man?

NO!

There is a polar bear in the snow.

Where is he going?

He is going to the sea!

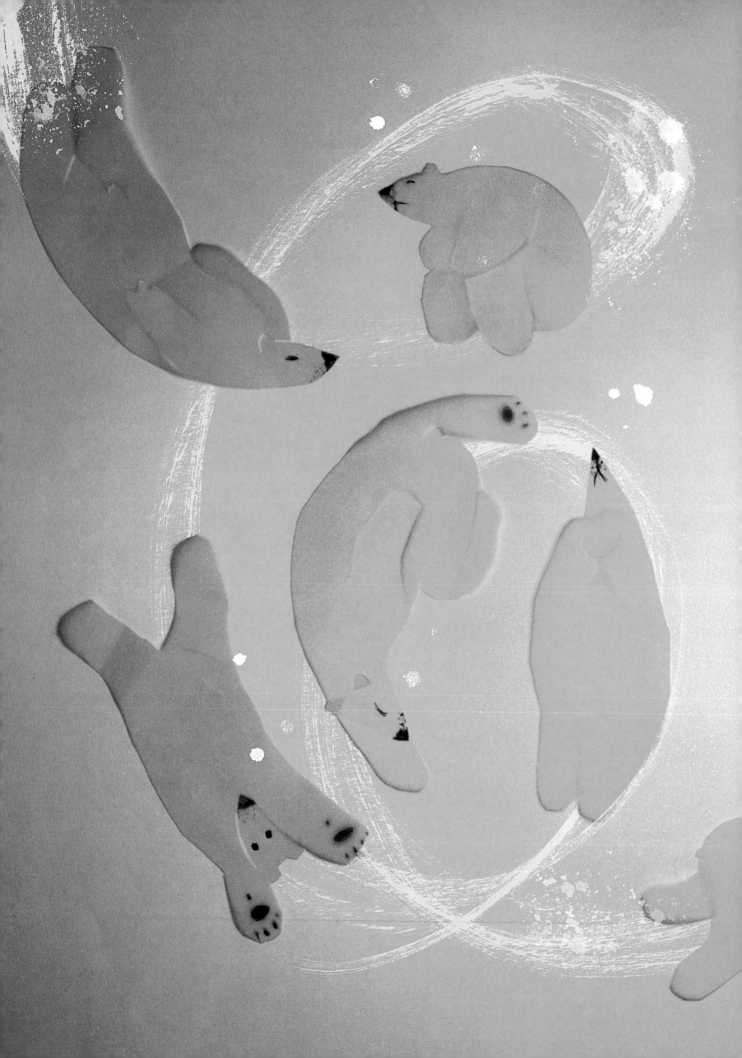

He wants to play.

And when he is done playing,

and he climbs back onto the snow,

where will he go then?

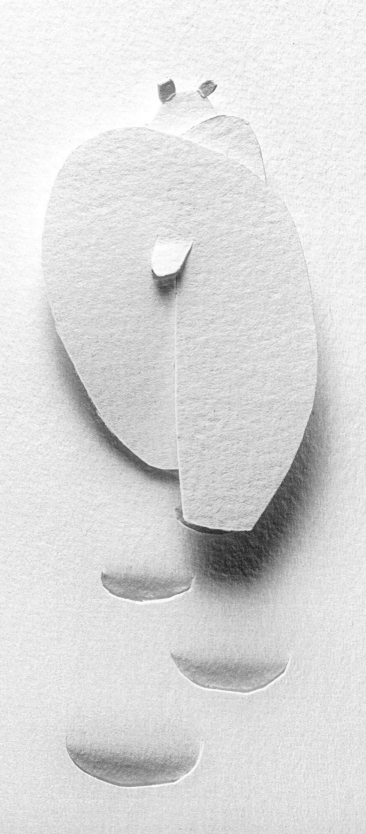

Who knows?